Sir Lewis Morris

Gwen : a drama in monologue in six acts

Sir Lewis Morris

Gwen : a drama in monologue in six acts

ISBN/EAN: 9783337304676

Printed in Europe, USA, Canada, Australia, Japan

Cover: Foto ©Andreas Hilbeck / pixelio.de

More available books at **www.hansebooks.com**

GWEN

A DRAMA IN MONOLOGUE

IN SIX ACTS

BY THE AUTHOR OF

"THE EPIC OF HADES"

" Everything is so wonderful, great and holy, so sad and yet
not bitter, so full of Death, and so bordering on Heaven."—JOHN
STERLING in Carlyle's Life.

LONDON
C. KEGAN PAUL & CO., 1, PATERNOSTER SQUARE
1879

TO HIS FRIEND

THE RIGHT HONOURABLE

JOHN BRIGHT, M.P.,

THIS POEM IS GRATEFULLY DEDICATED

BY

THE AUTHOR.

PREFACE.

—◦◦◦—

THE following poem is, as things now are, so far removed from the possibility of representation on the stage, that it seems needless to apologise for its wide departure from all the traditions of the acted drama.

The use of monologue is due to the fact that the writer has found it easier by this method to ensure to his characters the full expression of their inner selves than by subjecting them to the necessary limitations and frequent trivialities of dialogue.

It will be observed that the characters in Act VI. are not those of the rest of the poem.

December, 1878.

G W E N.

PROLOGUE.

Not of old time alone
Was Life a scene of hopes and fears,
High joys and bitter tears;
Nor Chance nor Fate are done;
Nor from our fuller Day
The fabled gods have wholly fled away;
The World and Man to-day are young
As when blind Homer sung.

What if the old forms change?

They were but forms, the things remain.

What if our fear and pain

Show not like monsters strange?

The self-same path of life

We tread, who fare beneath the sun to-day;

We sink or triumph in the strife

No otherwise than they.

Compact of good and ill

Their life of old was, as is ours;

The same mysterious Will

Controlled their finite powers;

And to strange thoughts of Fate

And workings of a fixed Necessity

Which rules both small and great,

As they bowed, so bow we.

And Love, the Lord and King—

Not Eros, but diviner far—

Still upon heavenward wing

Mounts like a shining star.

Than clouds and thunders stronger,

He brings a clear ray from the invisible Sun ;

And when he shines no longer,

Life's play is done.

ERRATA.

Page 24, line 7, *for* "rain or wind," *read* "wind or rain."

Page 148, line 3, *dele* "all."

ACT I.

B

SCENE I.

HENRY.

The sweet cold air of these untrodden hills
Breathes gently.   From the bustle of the inn
I turn refreshed to this free mountain-side,
And listen to the innumerable sound
Of the loud brook beneath, which roars and spumes
Brown-white against the granite.   These thick firs
Shed balm upon the evening air; there comes
No footstep but the rabbit's or the shrew's
Upon this grassy path, which winds and winds
Around the hill-side, under promontories
Of gold and purple, to the grey old church,

Where, chancing yesterday at eve, I caught

The sound of hymns, richer and fuller far

Than those of yore ; and, hidden within the porch,

Heard the prayers rising in a tongue unknown,

But musical as Greek ; and not unmoved

Watched the loud preacher, firing with his theme,

Grow rhythmic, and the answering moans which showed

He touched the peasant heart.

      Ah, it was long

Since I had heard men pray.   I have seen the cloud

Of incense rolling to the fretted roofs

Of dim cathedrals in the fair old lands

Where Faith weds not with Reason ; I have heard

The Benediction service, pure and sweet,

Lit by young voices ; I have watched with fear

In college aisles the polished, delicate priest

Poise his smooth periods on the razor edge

Of a too fine-drawn logic ; I have stood

And listened all unmoved, or all ashamed

That I was moved a little, by the trick

And artifice of speech which, though I knew it,

Could cheat the heart a moment, while the preacher

Enchained his ignorant thousands.   None of these

Moved me as that unknown tongue yesterday.

I thought my faith reviving.   Tush ! what folly !

That died long years ago from the roots, dried up

By the strong glare of knowledge, nor could aught

Of all the miracles the Churchmen feign

E'er water it to life.   That died long since,

Killed dead by German learning and the strong

And arrogant Priests of Science.   Yet God knows—

If God there be—I would give my life to know

The strong Belief of old, when little hands

Were folded morn and eve, and little eyes

Scarce open from the night, or half weighed down

By the long hours of play, were raised to see

Heaven in a mother's gaze.

                I would my soul
Might cast from it the dead unlovely load
Of dead men's speculations, rottennesses
Born of unloving lives which took the cell
And cloister for the home, and the midnight lamp
For the glow of the hearth, and palsied limbs of doubt
For the father's stalwart stride.   I am young still;
Yet often, when the flash of racing oars,
The shouts, the rushing feet, the joyous noise,
Floated among the avenues at eve
To my still college chamber; there would come
A weariness, a surfeit, a distaste
Of all the painted show which men call life,
Of all the sensual flush which men call love,
Of all the hollow, vain logomachies
Men take for learning, and I seemed to live
In premature decay, and to have touched

The fruit of life with eager lips and found it

Crumble away in dust.   And yet I know,

How little 'tis my few laborious years

Have given me of learning that might take

The utmost space of our allotted years,

Yet leave us still unquenched.   And yet what bar—

But seven little years—is there that parts

Me and my boyhood ?   Seven little years !

And still I am a youth in frame, in mind,

In innocence of harm of thought or deed,

In scorn of wrong, and of the sensual stye

Wherein the boor lies bound.   Only some power

There is which holds me fast and binds my will ;

Only some dim and paralyzing force

Freezes the springs of action, till I lie

Moored in some tideless and forgotten creek,

A ship which lies and rots ; while on high sea

The salt winds blow, the white crests break, the sail,

Filled with the stress of hope and youth and act,

Speeds to the unseen harbour.

               What shall cure

This sickness of the soul?　I would that I

Were like that peasant lad whom yester-eve

I saw—a stalwart boy, on whose red cheek

Scant sign of manhood showed; whose strong arm wound

Around his sweetheart's waist, as free from shame,

While down the village street they loitered slow

As 'twere the end of life to grow and breed

And die, as do his herds.　Yet here again

I hesitate to act, because I know

What love is in its cause, what in its end,

And by what secret, miry paths full oft

The winged god steals, when all his violet plumes

Are smirched with foulness, and his fair eyes droop,

Cloyed with the grosser sweets of lower earth,

And the keen arrow flies not through the skies,

But drops a blunted shaft.

                  I would I knew

Less, or grew wiser, knowing.   Golden hair,

Sweet eyes, the lithe young form, the girlish voice

Which issues forth so soft from the red lips

Arched like the bow of Cupid, the soft neck

Like a white pillar ; these were charms enow

I warrant, which might draw as by a spell

The rustic youth around.   Yes, she was fair

And sweet to see, and better, from her eyes

A pure young soul looked forth, which was well housed

Within so pure a body.—" Gwen " he called her—

'Tis a fair name—when by the vicarage gate

Her father stayed a moment courteously

To greet the stranger, and her shy glance turned

And met my tell-tale eyes.   Surely a man

Who had seen the hollowness of things might here

Dwell not unhappy—purple hills around,

And great tranquillity—a wife's sweet smile

Beside him ; little hands to draw him back

To the kindly earth ; and all the healthy load

Of daily liturgies which make a heaven

Of earth, and doubt a madness.

                      Tush ! what folly

Is this?   Have I not passed these things and spurned

The weakness from me—I, who have given years

Of youth to learning, and am tired a while

Of my mistress, nothing more?

                    And yet, what hope

Was it that brought me hither, this last night

I spend among the mountains?   Was it to watch

The sunset glories smite the golden sea,

Or hear the fairy rivulet fall in foam

Among the pines?   Or was it that I thought

Perchance a slender form might pass this way,

Crowned with the crown of youth, and a sweet voice

Answer my eager greeting?   Oh, what fools

And hypocrites are we, when a strong Power

Within us, unsuspected, binds us fast

And guides our footsteps !   It was not the face

Of outward nature, but the secret spring

Which sets our Being to a hidden end,

And bears the name of Love.

                        A gleam of blue,

A hat white-plumed—there is no other form

As graceful; it is she.   I may not love,

Who cannot wed.   I shall not see her more.

I am young still; I will but look a moment

In those young eyes, and hear that sweet young voice

Refine our common English, and to-morrow

She will forget the stranger who was kind,

And I the mountain-nymph who was so fair.

SCENE II.

I know not why my books,

The learning that I loved, the charm of art,

Should for a young girl's looks

Fade from my thought and vanish and depart.

It was but yesterday

I loved to pore upon the classic page

From morn to eve, nor could the damsels gay,

Who from the parching town

Flock to these pure cool heights, move me at all.

'Twas rest enough to roam

On the hill-side contented all day long,

And watch the shadows come

O'er moor and hill and purple wastes of sea ;

To see the evening fall

On breathless hill and dale, till suddenly

The pale moon rose ; then wander homeward slow

To my loved books with cheek with health aglow.

And now nor hill, nor dale, nor sea,

Nor the old task sufficeth me.

For two days since, ere night could fall,

There came a young girl eighteen summers old—

A simple girl, half peasant, lithe and tall,

With deep-blue eyes and hair of gold ;

And straightway my philosophy,

My learning, all forsaking me,

Left me a love-sick boy—no more—

Me who have drunk so deep of wiser lore !

Too wise, I thought, to rest content

With any childish blandishment ;
Too wise ! ah fool ! for looking in such eyes,
'Twere folly to be wise.

For as she tripped round the hill
To visit some cottage lowly,
With her basket of food on her arm,
She showed like Artemis holy ;
And I doffed to her, and she knew
The stranger of yesternight,
And her soft eyes showed more blue
As the rose on her cheek grew bright;
And, some power impelling me, I—
I who was always counted so shy—
I walked by her side a little, though I know
That my tongue was tied and my brain was slow ;
But however it was, yet her eyes were blue,
And her roses all aglow.

And I walked by her side till she came

To the cottage door, where we parted,

And a mingling of pride and of shame

Rose and left me awhile half-hearted.

I to stoop to a simple girl,

The child of a peasant sire !

Though the gown of the clergyman hides many faults,

Surely 'twas mine to aspire.

What would they say—my friends,

The pale students, polished and proud,

If I, the first of them, stooped to take

A wife from the vulgar crowd?

Or she, my dear mother, whose pride

Lies hid so deep in the depths of her heart,

There is scarcely one of us knows it is there ?

Or my father, the Earl, to whom life is no more

Than a long procession of hound and horse,

To whom hardly dishonour itself seems worse
Than to wed out of one's degree?

And I wandered out over the hill
For an hour of doubt or more,
And then, as it happened, my feet drew near
To that humble cottage door;
And I saw her come forth with a child on her arm,
Pale-faced and hollow-eyed,
And she seemed a pagan goddess no more,
But a fair Madonna, with all the charm
Of the Sistine or of the Chair.

And then, as over the hill
We walked back again, though her voice was still,
Surely was never a man so full
Of chattering talk as I.
But she was not angry at all, not she;

But from that calm vantage of wise eighteen,

And with only a modest word or so,

And a sweet voice, and musical accent low,

She would bend her delicate ear to me,

And listen, as grave and as calm as a queen,

To the talk which meant little enough, maybe,

But was understood, I ween.

But however it was, I know

When we came to the gate, and her little hand

Slid shyly out, as she wished me good-bye,

That as I turned to go

My feet seemed winged on the slope of the hills,

And I hardly knew that the cold half-sleet

Which blots the clouded mountain and chills

The unsheltered wayfarer, wrapping me round,

Had drenched me.   For up the silent street

Of the darkling village, jubilant sound

Compassed me ; sunlight beamed on me still ;

And even to my high inn-chamber I seemed

To be treading that breezy hill.

What is the charm which wakes

The bud, the flower, the fruit, from the cold ground?

What is the power which makes

With song the groves, with song the fields, resound ?

One spell there is, so strong to move ;

Some call it Spring, and others Love.

I thought my heart lay dead—

Sad heart, long buried deep in dusty lore !—

But now, the winter fled,

It beats with quicker beat than e'er before.—

A simple girl, yet can she move

Spring in my soul, the Spring of Love !

Strange fable that they taught

Of old, of souls divided as in twain,

Each by the other sought

Until the sundered reunite again,

And then the severed members move,

Knit by the magic spell of Love !

Ah, let us be at one,

Dear soul, if one we be, and are of kin

Before the world begun ;

Sure 'tis that I was made thy soul to win.

Ah, child, if we might upward move,

Borne on the golden wings of Love !

SCENE III.

What is it the village leech

Tells me of fever and chill,

And bids me keep warm ?   Well, it perhaps were wise ;

For I fail to sleep, and my limbs are as lead,

And a throb of painfulness splits my head,

And they warned me of this, I remember, again and

    again.

But surely I know that, came rain or wind,

If only my weary limbs could reach

To that little gate on the breezy hill

And I saw the desire of my eyes,

I should take little thought of myself, not I,

Not even were I doomed to die.

SCENE IV.

What is this? And where am I?

This is not the high inn-chamber, I know,

This white little room where the sunset-glow

On the white bed-curtains, as I lie,

Makes orange shadows which fade and fleet ;

Nor are these my first nurse's reluctant feet

Which steal so lightly and daintily round,

As if grudging the faintest ghost of a sound ;

Nor was the soft voice I heard

Last night, when the curtain was silently stirred,

The village doctor's at all :

I have heard it before, but when, I cannot recall.

For there comes a sense on my brain

Of time that is gone but has left no trace

But days which passed and left nothing behind,

Yet upon the secret depths of the mind

Are graven that nought may erase.

As the patient metal retains the sound

Of the living voice that is dead, ,

Even so doth my being retain

A long procession of days and nights,

Weary and suffering and heavily sped;

And then for a moment the cool air strikes,

As some one carries me tenderly down,

And slowly the wheels of my litter climb,

Leaving the streets of the little town,

Up the hill through the scented pines.

And then all is blank for a time ;

A long time, surely, when nothing came

But wandering dreams and a whispered name,

Repeated often and like a charm,

To keep off fancied phantoms of harm.

" Gwen," was it ?　Somewhere I seem to recall,

Far away in some world of forgotten things,

A fair young face which I loved to see ;

And one night in this room it smiled on me,

And the ghastly shapes spread their horrible wings

And left me at rest for a while.

Ah, no ! I did not dream it at all,

For now for a week she comes every day,

A young nurse, virginal, white, and tall,

And her father, the vicar, whose rough face beams

With a genial kindness he cannot speak ;

For if ever he ventures a word, it is gall

To one who is peevish and weak,

And his words struggle out like stones in a stream,

Jerked together, and jostled, and battered away,

Till I long that he had done.

But she, my Artemis pure and fair,

My Madonna, who stood at the cottage gate—

She is perfect, I hold, from the crown of her hair

To the dainty sole of her delicate foot ;

And her hand and her voice are as soft as silk,

And she comes hour by hour with a tender care,

With my draught or my food, or with rich cool milk.

Ah ! if only—— What, am I then worse than the brute,

That I stoop to thoughts that I loathe and hate—

I, a great peer's only son ?

For I see on the walls of my simple room,

Which I know was her own, the work of her hand,

At night, in the firelight's flickering gloom,

This text emblazoned in letters of gold—

" For whom Christ dièd." Ah, if indeed

His words were the words of a real doom,

And his faith the faith of a living creed !

But now souls and beliefs are bargained and sold,

There is no belief by which men may stand,

There is neither creed nor God.

But whether there be or be not indeed,

It shall not change me or move my mind.

Shall I who hate to see weak things bleed,

From the hare which shrieks, to the trout on the hook.

Play false with the simple heart of a maid,

Till her poor soul pines for a new-born need?

I dare not do it; I am afraid

To see the young soul, with a terrible look,

Go out for the truth which it cannot find

By dark ways, of truth untrod.

She shall keep unassailed her young innocent heart,

For aught to be whispered by me or done;

She shall hold her faith; but 'tis best we part,

For hearts break daily and white lives fade,

And 'twere better indeed I had never been born,

Than to bring a young life to sorrow and woe,

And leave a pure saint to the cold world's scorn,

Shrinking back from the wreck which myself had made.

No, of all the wrong-doing beneath the sun,

Not this one be mine, oh God !

White room ! white curtain ! little bed

That once was hers, whereon she lay

So warm and still, her sunny head

Safe pillowed till the growing day !

I bless you and I love you all.

I feel so young who once seemed old.

I see a lithe girl-figure, tall,

With grave blue eyes and hair of gold,

Stand by the half-closed door when he,

The village doctor, yesternight,

Came stealthily and looked on me,
With noiseless step and shaded light ;

And I, who in a lethargy
Seemed buried, to a careless eye,
Lay all unmoved, till suddenly
I caught the echo of a sigh,

And, looking up, beheld my dear,
The first love of my weary heart,
Stand pitiful, and marked the tear
In the soft eye unbidden start.

Yet no prognostics dire they were
He launched against me ; only these :
Torpor and weakness, needing care
And watchfulness for remedies ;

And, seeing that I saw and heard,
Turned to me with a cheerful face,
And spoke some random hopeful word,
And nodded smiling to the place,

Where stood the stair.   But I, I knew
A sudden rush of hope and strength,
And cared not when, if but at length,
My new-born thought should turn out true.

SCENE V.

Oh, joy ! I grow stronger day by day ;

And day by day in the sweet summer weather

I wander over the hills, and away

High up 'mid the purple masses of heather,

Till mounting aloft with no one by,

All in the bountiful summer weather,

I drink in new life from every pore,

Throbbing and bourgeoning more and more

In every limb and with every breath,

As, laid on the heather, I watch the sky

And the purple shadows on sea and hill,

And hear no sound but the bee's deep hum,

And watch the shy mountain-sheep timidly come,

And the kestrel circling, aloft on the rocky brow,

Fulfilling the marvellous mission of Death and of Pain.

Death ! ah, but that is far from me now,

Vanished with Pain and its legions of Ill.

I can walk with my limbs, I can leap, I can run ;

I rejoice in my strength : the day of weakness is done.

I live, I grow strong ; I am one with the World and with
     Life again.

And sometimes, rare blessing, there comes with me

A fair young Oread over the hill,

Fearless and free from a thought of ill.

For her mother, who came of gentler blood,

Who was always delicate, kind, and good—

Her mother died long ago, and she

Has lived from her childhood fearless and free.

I think no thought of passion as yet

Has touched her.   Only pity made wet

Her eyes on that night which awoke my love.

I am only a friend more mature and wise

Than any she knows, and a shamed surprise

Would wake in the sapphire depths of her eyes,

If she saw what blind and passionate longings move

Within the hidden thoughts of a man.

Ah, well ! but nature is twofold, and sure

It were not wise to ban

The instincts which are neither gross nor pure.

Let him suppress them who can.

It is only in thought I invade her virginal peace,

For I know that this sweet rehearsal of love must cease.

For I am not my own ; but my wife to be,

Stately and beautiful, waits for me

With that which suffices to build up our shattered wealth.

Ay, but what if love, awaking and coming by stealth,

D

Should bind me in chains on this wild Welsh hill?

Or hurry me downward, downward, to fathomless ill?

Tush! how should I be a devil if there be not a God?

I am only a young man in whom the young blood

Pulses quickly, and have I no gratitude

For the life which she saved, the life which is grown so
sweet,

As we roam o'er these breeze-swept uplands with rapid
young feet?

Oh, joy! I am one with the life of the hills, and the skies,
and of man!

SCENE VI.

It is done ! I have told her I love her,

Yester-eve as we walked together,

Some power grown tyrannous holding me fast,

Blotting alike the Future and Past ;

And for answer she gave but a sigh and a start,

And a blush as bright as the purple heather,

And a little flutter of bosom and heart,

And a glow like the hues of the sunset above her.

Oh, fair ash-grove where I told my love !

Fair ash-grove dear to Cymric verse

Since their bard who sang thee when Chaucer was
    young !

Fairest of groves that were ever sung !

Oh, fairest sunset of all that have shone

Since man first woke in Paradise garden,

Before the temptation, the ruin, the curse,

Before the strange story was over and done,

And man an outcast hopeless of pardon !

As we sat on the mossy bank, she and I,

And no creature was near with intrusive eye,

To mark our innocent joy !

Sweet day when love awakens and stands,

With his free limbs bare and his stretched-out hands.

Before two young shame-fast natures which yearn

With innocent yearning : clear fires that burn

Free from all baser alloy.

It is done ; it is over; and never Eve,

The mother of maidens who love and grieve,

Looked fairer than did Gwen,

This peasant maiden, when first she heard

The one ineffable, passionate word

Which stirs for ever the hearts of maidens and of men.

The bud on the bough,

The song of the bird,

The blue river-reaches

By soft breezes stirred ;

Oh, soul, and hast thou found again thy
treasure ?

Oh, world, and art thou once more filled
with pleasure ?

Oh, world, hast thou passed

Thy sad winter again ?

Oh, soul, hast thou cast

Thy dull vesture of pain ?

Oh ! winter, sad wert thou and full of sorrow ;

Oh soul, oh world, the summer comes to-morrow !

Oh, soul ! 'tis love quickens

Time's languorous feet ;

Oh, world ! 'tis Spring wakens

Thy fair blossoms sweet ;

Fair world, fair soul, that lie so close together,

 Each with sad wintry days and fair Spring weather !

As on the clear hill-sides we walked together,

A gleam of purple passed over the sea,

And, glad with the joy of the summer weather,

My love turned quickly and looked on me.

Ah, the glad summer weather, the fair summer weather !

Ah, the purple shadow on hill and sea !

And I looked in her eyes as we walked together,

And knew the shy secret she fain would hide,

And we went hand in hand through the blossoming

    heather,

She who now was my sweetheart, and I by her side ;

For the shade was the shadow of Love's wing-feather,

Which bares, as he rises, the secrets we hide.

Now, come cloud or sunshine, come joy or weeping,

It can be no longer as 'twas before.

Just a shadow of change o'er the soul comes creeping,

And farewell to the joyaunce and freedom of yore ;

For it crosses Love's face, where he lies a-sleeping,

And he soars awaking, nor slumbers more.

I have found her !

At last, after long wanderings, dull delays,

I have found her ;

And all my life is tuned to joy and praise.

I have found her !

A myriad-myriad times

In man's long history this thing has been ;

All ages, climes,

This daily, hourly miracle have seen

A myriad-myriad times ;

Yet is it new to-day.

I have found her, and a new spring glads my eyes.

　World, fair and gay

As when Eve woke in dewy Paradise,

　Fade not away !

　Fade not, oh light,

Lighting the eyes of yet another pair,

　But let my sight

Find her as I have found her, pure and fair !

　Shine, mystic light !

Yes, it is sweet to be
Awaited, and to know another heart
Beats faster for our coming, and to see
The blush unbidden start
To the fair cheek, and mark young Love's alarms
Perturb and make more fair the girlish charms.

I am once more
A young man with the passions of my kind ;
I am no pedant, glorying as before
In barren realms of mind.
The springtide that awakens land and sea,
The Spring of Youth and Love, awakens me.

It calls, and all my life

Answers from its dim depths, "I come, I hear."

It breaks, it bursts, in sudden hope and strife,

And precious chills of fear.

It comes with tremulous, furtive thrills which can

Strip from me all the Past, and leave me, man.

SCENE VII.

GWEN.

Dear hills, dear vales, how calm and bright

Ye show in morning's early light !

Dear woods and uplands cool and wild,

Where yesterday I walked a child,

I love you, but I roam no more

With all the careless joy of yore.

My girlish days are past and done ;

I know my womanhood begun.

What was it one so wise could see

In an untutored child like me?

What was it?   Nay, 'twere sin to prove
By earthy tests the ways of love.
Whate'er it was, Love's perfect way
Is without doubting to obey.

I do obey.   I lay my soul
Low at Love's feet for his control.
Farewell, oh paths half hidden in flowers,
Trodden by young feet in childish hours;
White bed, white room, and girlish home !
The hour of Love and Life is come !

I shall not watch as yesterday
The orange sunset fade to gray,
Nor roam unfettered as the bee,
A maiden heart and fancy free.
I am bound by such a precious chain
I may not wander forth again.

Oh, bond divine ! oh, sweet, sweet chain !

Oh, mingling of ecstatic pain !

I am a simple girl no more.

I would not have it as before.

One day of love, one brief, sweet day,

And all my past is swept away.

Oh, vermeil rose and sweet,

Rose with the golden heart of hidden fire,

Bear thou my yearning soul to him I love.

Bear thou my longing and desire.

Glide safe, oh sweet, sweet rose,

By fairy-fall and cliff and mimic strand,

To where he muses by the sleeping stream.

Then eddy to his hand.

Drown not, oh vermeil rose,
But from thy dewy petals let a tear
Fall soft for joy when thou shalt know the touch
And presence of my dear.

Tell him, oh sweet, sweet rose,
That I grow fixed no more, nor flourish now
In the sweet maiden garden-ground of old,
But severed even as thou.

Say from thy golden heart,
From virgin folded leaf and odorous breath,
That I am his to wear or cast away,
His own in life or death.

Thy shadow, oh tardy night,

Creeps onward by valley and hill,

And scarce to my straining sight

Show the white road-reaches still.

Oh, night, stay now a little, little space,

And let me see the light of my beloved's face !

My love is late, oh night,

And what has kept him away ?

For I know that he takes not delight

In the garish joys of day.

Haste, night, dear night that bring'st my love to me !

What if his footsteps halt and tarry but for thee ?

E

Nay, what if his footsteps slide

By the swaying bridge of pine,

And whirled seaward by the tide

Is the loved form I counted mine !

Oh, night, dear night that comest yet dost not come,

How shall I wait the hour that brings my darling home?

Fair star that on the shoulder of yon hill

Peepest, a little eye of tranquil night,

Come forth.   Nor sun nor moon there is to kill

Thy ray with broader light.

Shine, star of eve that art so bright and clear ;

Shine, little star, and bring my lover here !

My lover! oh, fair word for maid to hear!

My lover who was yesterday my friend!

Oh, strange we did not know before how near

Our stream of life smoothed to its fated end!

Shine, star of eve, as Love's self, bright and clear;

Shine, little star, and bring my lover here!

He comes! I hear the echo of his feet.

He comes! I fear to stay, I cannot go.

Oh, Love, that thou art shame-fast, bitter-sweet,

Mingled with pain, and conversant with woe!

Shine, star of eve, more bright as night draws near;

Shine, little star, and bring my lover here!

What shall I do for my love,

Who is so tender

And dear and true,

Loving and true and tender,

My strength and my defender —

What shall I do?

I will cleave unto my love,

Who am too lowly

For him to take.

With a self-surrender holy

I will cleave unto him solely ;

I will give my being wholly

For his dear sake.

ACT II.

SCENE I.

HENRY.

Only a little week

Of meetings under the star,

Since the blissful evening I dared to speak,

Sweet evening that seems so far !

And already the cruel post brings me word

That my mother the countess, who, far away

At a German bath with her ailing lord,

Has been dreaming the early autumn away,

Returns to-day, and to-morrow will come

To take the invalid leisurely home.

Ah, mother! I fear that your pride will scorn

That your son should mate with a lowly bride,

Though a vicar's daughter is well enough born

For all but a foolish pride.

And I know, moreover, your heart is set

On her to whom no word is spoken yet,

The lofty heiress who comes to restore

Our house to the splendours of yore.

Poor mother, your patience was sadly tried

By the studious fancies which kept me apart

From the London which now seems to hold your heart;

And, alas! I hardly know how to face

The blank amaze of your haughty gaze,

The cold surprise of patrician eyes,

As you listen to my disgrace.

Disgrace, did I say? Ah! where

In all the bewildering town

Is any as Gwen is, fair

Or comely, or high or pure?

Or when did a countess's coronet crown

A head with a brighter glory of hair?

Or how could titular rank insure

A mind and a heart so sweet?

They shall not shame me to cheat or beguile

My darling, my queen, my treasure,

Nor blot from my soul the pure pleasure

Of the brief hours that have been.

And if indeed I must go for a while,

It shall not be for long, but a little while ;

And then I will haste back again with passionate feet,

To bask again in her smile.

I must tell her all to-night, sweet to-night, when we meet.

SCENE II.

I have seen her once again,

I have seen her again, my dear.

And oh, but parting was a bitter pain!

And oh, the ready, child-like tear!

I did not know, even I, before,

With how immense and ponderous a chain

Love binds the girlish heart, and holds it evermore.

For I hardly know at all

How it came to be, but as we two spoke

Of parting and absence her sweet voice broke,

And she paled and wavered as if to fall ;

And 'twas only a ready encircling arm,

And lip to lip in a close embrace,

That brought back the rose to her troubled face,

And recalled the wandering life from its swift alarm.

Dear young soul that Fate has given me to hold,

And shall I forsake thee, come weal or woe ?

No, I will not betray thy sweet trustfulness ; no,

Not for millions of gems and gold.

But before I left her and went

My way to the inn, while the village street

Echoed loud with the rhythmical wheels and feet

Of my mother's chariot, we vowed together

That, whatever the changes of life and weather,

We would cling to each other and never part ;

And so I, the round of festivities done,

And the pheasants all killed and the county won,

Will steal from my gilded trammels, and come
To the Welsh hillside which is now my home,
And the child who has my heart.

Was ever a girlish heart so fair
As Gwen's, or free from earth?
She is pure and innocent, I swear,
As an infant at the birth.
She is full, indeed, of much old-world lore,
From the lessons her mother taught her of yore ;
Mozart's sweet melodies loves to rehearse,
And many a tome of forgotten verse ;
And something of modern letters she knows,

And oft in fancy with Elaine goes,

As she floateth lifeless to Camelot.

But of wrong and evil she knoweth not.

She knows no more of the ways of men,

Their deceits, their treacheries,

Or of coarse, bold women,—my little Gwen,

With the clear, deep, trusting eyes—

Than if you should come by some Arctic main,

Where a world of ice shuts humanity out ;

On some simple forgotten colony,

Which had never heard of the world or wealth;

Or a convent set on a scarpèd hill.

Tush ! but they would corrupt each other, no doubt,

Or some echo of evil would creep in by stealth.

But for Gwen the pure cold stream of her will

Flows along the mountain-side, taking no stain,

Crystal-clear, reflecting its kindred sky.

Was ever a soul so fair ?

Forget me not, dear soul ! Yet wherefore speak
The words of freedom, where the thing is not ?
Forget me not ! And yet how poor and weak
My prayer, who know that nothing is forgot !
Low voice, or kindling eye, or glowing cheek,
Forget them not !

Forget me only if forgetting prove
Oblivion of low aims and earthy thought ;
Forget the blinder appetites which move
Through secret ways, by lower nature taught ;
Forget them, love !

Remember only, with fond memory,

The exaltation, the awakened soul,

Swift moments strong to bind my heart to thee,

Strong tides of passionate faith which scorn control—

In these remember me !

Dear child so sweet in maidenhood,

How should I doubt, regarding thee,

A secret spring of hidden Good,

Which rules all things and bids them be ?

Dear soul, so guileless and so pure,

So innocent and free from stain,

As 'twere untempted Eve again,
I lean upon thee and grow sure.

I love no more the barren quest,
The doubt I cherished I despise ;
I am a little while at rest,
Seeing the Godhead in thine eyes.

Can good be, yet no Giver?   Can
The stream flow on, yet own no source?
From what deep well of hidden Force
Flows the diviner stream in man ?

I know not.   Some there is, 'tis clear,
A mystery of mysteries.
Thy youth has gazed upon it, dear,
And bears its image in thine eyes.

Yes, God there is.   Too far to know,

It may be, yet directing all.

It is enough ; we spring, we grow,

We ripen, we decay, we fall,

To a great Will.   No empty show

Of aimless and unmeaning ends

Our life is, but the overflow

Of a great Spring which always tends

To a great Deep.   The silver thread

Between the Fountain and the Sea

We are for ever, quick or dead,

And Source and Ending both are He.

It is enough—no more I know;

But maybe from thy faithful eyes,

F

Thy trust that knows no chill, thy glow

Of meek and daily sacrifice,

I may relearn the legend fair

I whispered at my mother's keee,

And seeing Godhead everywhere,

Confess, "And this man too was He."

SCENE III.

GWEN.

Oh, happy days so lately done,

And yet removed so far away,

Before our passion-tide begun

And life's young May !

Shy early days of sun and showers,

When all the paths were hidden in flowers

Tender and sweet,

And on the mountain-side the year,

With girlish change of smile and tear,

Tripped with light feet ;

And by the melting snows the violet came,

And on the wolds the crocus like a saffron flame !

Daily some song of lonely bird,

By tufted field or tasselled grove,

From the clear dawn to solemn eve was heard,

But few of love.

Nay, rather virginal flutings pure and clear,

Passionless preludes, ah, how dear !

Nor yet upon the nest,

The bright-eyed fearless mother sate,

Nor yet high in mid-heaven her soaring mate

Thrilled his full breast,

Nor yet within the white domain of song

Love burst with eyes aglow the maiden choir among.

But when the fuller summer shone,

Soon as the perfumed rose had come,

Lo, all the reign of song was done,

The birds all dumb ;

And for the choir which did before rejoice,

Low, tuneless accents of an anxious voice

Weighed down with care,

And dim forebodings choking the high note

Which once resounded from the joyous throat

So full and fair.

I would not lose my love which is so dear,

But 'tis oh the parted days of the imperfect year !

Oh, soft dove gently cooing

To thy mate upon her nest,

And hast thou known undoing

And deep unrest?

And does any pain of wooing

Wring thy soft breast?

Oh, pale flower ever turning

To thy great lord the sun,

And dost thou know a yearning

Which is never done,

For the tardy summer burning

And June begun?

Ah, heart ! there is no pleasure

As thine, nor grief.

Time Future holds the treasure;

Time Past, the thief.

What power brings this one, measure.

Or that, relief?

Ah ! 'tis not very long

Since I was light and free,

And of all the burden of pain and wrong

No echo reached to me ;

But day by day, upon this breeze-swept hill,

Far from the too great load of human ill,

I lived within the sober walls of home,

Safe-set, nor heard the sound of outward evil come.

It is not that I know,

By word or any deed,

What depths of misery lie below,

What hearts that bleed ;

But, since I have felt the music of my soul

Touched by another's mastering hand,

I seem to hear unfathomed oceans roll,

As when a child I saw the Atlantic lash the strand.

Oh, mother, who art dead

So long beneath the grass,

Lift up once more, lift thy beloved head

When we two pass,

And tell me—tell me if this passionate pain,

This longing, this ineffable desire

For one I know so lately, be the gain

To which young maids aspire.

Is this to love, to kiss my chain and feel

A dominant will to which 'tis joy to kneel?

Oh, mother, I am a maid;

I am young, I know not men.

My great joy makes me shrink and be afraid.

It is not now as then

When first we walked together on the hill.

I take no longer, thought for any soul

Of those I loved before and cherish still;

I care not for the poor, the blind, the lame;

I care not for the organ's solemn roll,

Or sabbath hymn and prayers, who am burnt as of a flame.

Nay, love ! how can I doubt thee

Who art so dear,

Though I pine away without thee

In the fading year?

The ash flings down its leaf, the heather

Is bloomless in the autumn weather ;

The mountain paths are wet with rime,

Where we together eve by eve

Would wander in the joyous time,

Fair hours when thy returning strength

Came with the days' increasing length.

I pace alone the dear familiar road

Where first we met.   I walk alone ;

I have no aim nor purpose, none—

Only to think of those soft days and still believe.

Last evening, on a distant hill,

A wreath of cloud-mist dealing sleet

Compassed my homeward steps, as still

I toiled with weary feet.

Oh, what if the snow, like a winding-sheet,

Had stayed the steps of my life and my troubled will,

And closed on me for ever, concluding there

My little hopes and joys, and maybe my despair !

Nay, I will not doubt him nor be afraid ;

He is all that is good, I know it, tender and true.

But I fear he is higher in rank than he said ;

For one day, I remember it well, as he lay

Very weak on his bed, a letter came

Coronet-blazoned, and half in shame

I lifted my eyes, and he saw I knew,

And his face grew troubled and never more

Was his gaze as frank as it was before.

Tender it was, indeed, and ardent and true,

But not as frank as before.

But I count the days till he comes again;

I long for him with a dull, deep pain.

I will do whatever thing my love commands;

I will go or stay; I am taken as a bird in his hands.

Oh, love, my love! tarry not long;

I am not happy nor strong.

Delay not, love; the sun has lost his fire.

Stay not; the cold earth loses light and heat,

Summer is gone, and Winter with cold feet

Chills all the world's desire.

Come back, and coming bring back Spring with thee,

Spring for my heart though all the world lie dead;

My life will burst in blossom at thy tread—

Oh, love, come back to me !

ACT III.

SCENE I.

HENRY.

Once more upon these dear familiar hills
I tread; 'tis autumn now, 'twas summer then.
The valley paths are deep in mire; the leaf
Falls sadly from the bough; the village inn,
So noisy then, when four months since I lay
'Twixt life and death, is silent; a gray mist
Hangs o'er the breathless valley.   All the hills
Are clouded, on whose summits a thin cowl
Of snowflakes sits at times.   Summer is dead :
A sad autumnal stillness over all
The dull world broods, and in my heart I know
Summer is dead—sweet summer, ah, too brief!

                                                    G

For now, alas ! I know

What folly 'twas that kept me here

Three little months ago.

I have drunk deep since then of cups that cheer,

The sea of eyes, the beat of popular hands,

When to his thought the high-set platform reels,

As now the solitary speaker stands

Poised like a swimmer on high waves, who feels

The world cut off from him and knows

To fail is ruin.   I have known

Men better since, and felt how near

And yet far off are clown and peer ;

And known how better than all lore,

Better than love itself, and more,

How satisfying and how great,

It is to aid the ship of state,

The labouring ship which reels and goes

Athwart the ranks of watching foes.

And best of all I know

How baseless was my sweet Arcadian dream.

I could not bear—I know it well—

To live retired from the central stream

Of life, as if in a hermit's cell.

I long for the hurry, the passion, the glow

Of full life lived in the eyes of men ;

I can bear no longer to dream in inglorious ease.

A great name, the voice of the people, authority, these

Are more than my simple Gwen.

Ay, and I have learnt besides,

What I scarce suspected before,

By what poor expedients my father has striven

To keep the wolf from his door—

Bubble schemes, mine-ventures which came to nought,

And some senseless bet on some swindling race,

And I know not what gambling follies beside.

But I know that our lawyer, with long-drawn face,

Came to me with secret warnings of ill,

And hints that a prudent marriage alone could fill

The coffers so nearly empty, again.

Poor father ! it was not right, for your dreams of gain,

And your pompous life and wasteful, orderless state,

To diminish a family hoard that was never great ;

But I know that if the blow he hinted should come,

And the Jew and the broker harried our ancient home,

It would kill you and drive my mother distraught.

Nay, I could not bear to see it.   My path is clear ;

I must see you once more and leave you, my love, my

 dear.

SCENE II.

I did not know it, I swear;

I did not dream that a young girl, fair and free,

Could long care for one grave and studious and worn
    like me.

I thought our brief passion was dead;

I thought I had schooled my heart to obey my head;

But when I saw her, she showed so fair,—

It was just at the self-same spot where we used to meet,—

That I hastened up the steep path with wings to my feet;

And she did not see me at first, but stood for a while

Silent and musing and still, with a sweet half-smile,

As if bent on some mingled vision of joy and pain,

And I knew that our love was not dead, but slept and
awoke again.

But when at length she turned her eyes,

With a beautiful, pitiful look of surprise,

And a questing glance, and a shiver and a start,

Oh, 'twas then that she touched my heart !

And before a moment passes again we stand,

With eyes on each other bent, and hand linked to hand ;

And with hardly a spoken word, we are face to face,

Strained together again in a close embrace ;

And I failed, I failed to tell her what should have been
told,

For the heart of a maid is higher than rank or gold.

But to-night I must speak and tell her all,

I must tell her though the sky fall.

SCENE III.

It is over, it is done.

She from the clear frank depths of her maidenly pride :

" Dear, it is sudden indeed, but I thought it would come,

For I doubt if any are happy under the sun.

But you, you shall not imperil the pride of your home ;

I know you a fitting mate for a loftier bride.

I will love you and pray for you always.   And now
    good-bye.

Be good, my dear, to your wife.   But I

Have awoke from my dream in time, and will tend

My poor, who, I fear, have missed a friend ;

And my father is growing old, and will want me here.

Fear not, I shall not be unhappy.   Farewell, my dear !"

And she went with feet as swift as the bounding roe,

And vanished before I knew she was minded to go,

And left me alone with the dying day in the fading year.

I cannot leave her thus ; I must see her again,

Though I know it is cruel to both and renewal of pain.

But all night long have I lain awake,

Tossing and fevered for her dear sake,

As when she nursed me to life in her little room ;

And once, when I dozed a moment, I seemed to hear

Her sweet voice calling aloud in accents of fear,

Calling my name in a voice which sank to a moan ;

And, though I know it was dreaming fancy alone,

I cannot leave her thus.   I am harassed with fears ;

I must see her again ; I must write. And lo ! through the
	gloom

The slow dawn of autumn breaks in mist and in tears.

Dear, I must see you again.

Bring with you the last sweet rose

Which lingers still in your garden-ground,

The last red summer rose.

Do you mind how you sent me a rose

Along the swift streamlet's flow,

A sweet and a blushing rose?

It is faded—'twas long ago.

Come, dear.   A dream visited me

In the weary vigilant night;

I heard your voice calling to me

In grievous pain and affright.

I must see you.   The swift wheels stay

At the spot we have known of yore ;

Be there, ere they bear me away

From my love for evermore.

SCENE IV.

GWEN.

The light has gone out of my life,

Yet I will not repine.

Nay, 'tis well to have passed betimes through the struggle

    and strife.

Shall I grieve that he comes not again,

That my love is not mine?

Ah, folly! the whole creation travails in pain.

I will live my own life once more;

I will succour the weak;

I will be but a little more grave than I was before.

I will strive to repay the deep love

My fond father fails to speak ;

Though the path may be lonely and drear, yet the

heavens are above.

Ah ! my love who no longer art mine,

Yet my love till I die,

I will strive to be patient and strong, but I wither and

pine.

A letter from my love,

In the well-remembered hand,

Once again, yet we have parted ;

'Tis hard to understand.

A letter from my love !

Dear letter, and what says he ?

" I am going away for ever.

Come once more, dear to me,

"And with you bring a rose."—

My love, I will be there ;

I will bring you a red, red rosebud

Upon your heart to wear.

But you must not crush it, dear,

Or bind it to you too fast,

Or the poor flower's scent, I fear,

Will bring back to you the Past.

Wear your rose lightly, dear,

For ornament or pleasure ;

But the virgin rose of a maiden's heart

Keep safe as a precious treasure.

ACT IV.

H

SCENE I.

HENRY.

How weak are we and blind !

How ignorant of fate !

For I thought I was steadfast and firm, and knew my
  mind,

Till I saw her at the gate ;

And next day, as soon as the train rolled on and I sat
  alone,

I wished that I had not written to give her pain,

And I prayed that she might not come, nor might I see
  her again.

But when the swift wheels slackened and grew still

At the little wayside station beyond the hill,

There alone by the platform stood my treasure, my dear,

Very pale, with a rose in her hand ; full of maidenly fear.

And I sprang out to her, and we whispered ardent and
    low,

With sad hearts throbbing together and cheeks aglow,

For a precious minute or two, till the signal to go ;

And then, all my youth and my love rising up like a
    flame,

I whispered, " I cannot leave you, my love, my bride.

Come to me, my own, my wife !"

                      And lo ! as in a trance,

With a shiver and tottering limbs, and a pitiful glance,

As one who walked in a dream, she obeyed and came

Constrained, and sank fainting down in her place at my
    side.

There she lay long time on my breast, very pale and chill,

And I trembled to see her poor white face, my dear ;

And the swift train had sped us long miles, when, with
something of fear,

She said quickly, "Where am I?" And I: "With your
husband to be.

We are long miles away from your home. You will trust
me, my own?"

And she moaned, "Ah! how could I leave my father
alone?

Poor father! Ah! what will they think of me when they
know?

They will deem me unmaidenly—bold. Let me go. We
were mad;

It is nothing to women to wither and pine and be sad.

Let me go. It is better. Some weakness constrained
me to come.

I will go and be happy, fear not, with my equals at home."

But I soothed her, and flashed a message to say she was
well,

And to promise a letter next day, telling all that there

    was to tell ;

And she lay like a child on my heart, with her head bent

    wearily down,

And lo ! on the autumn twilight, the glare and the

    turmoil of town.

    I hold him wrong who opens wide

    The secret, sacred doors of love,

    The paths by shame-fast footsteps tried,

    The mazes of the enchanted grove.

I hold him wrong ; but Gwen my wife
Is dearer even than Gwen the maid.
We walk by hidden deeps of life,
And no man maketh us afraid.

I hold him wrong; but who can prize
At its full worth the love he gains,
Till bound by mutual sacrifice,
Till fused by mutual joys and pains?

Too happy are the halcyon days ;
For Time the taker, Time the thief,
Steals ghostlike down the flowery ways,
And makes the blessed moments brief.

I have left her ofttimes for a while,

And then, on some pretext hastily found,

Have hurried back to bask in her smile;

But now I am here fast bound,

For my father is failing, day by day,

And 'tis hard to keep the harpies at bay,

Who would enter and turn him from house and home.

They must not suspect that I, who am alone

The mainstay on which they depend to secure their own,

Am not the lover of one who brings lands and wealth,

But bound to a penniless girl whom I wedded by stealth;

They must not dream it; and therefore here must I stay,

Though I seem indeed to lose every day

That keeps me away from my love.

Dear soul, it is springtime again, and fresh currents move

Through the world, and stir the life in blossom and tree,

And the little hidden life which ere long shall be.

SCENE II.

GWEN.

Dear love, I will be patient, yet
I long to see you, and I fear
Lest absence lead you to forget
The things that once were dear.

You tell me we awhile must hide
Our union safe from prying eyes,
But when your ailing father dies
You will proclaim me as your bride.

I long that this might be, nor wait
The death of any.   I have been
These last six months, 'spite love and fate,
Dearest, as happy as a queen.

But now another dearer life
Forbids my careless patience more.
Pray God it may not come before
I am acknowledged for your wife.

I did not know,

When I walked careless on the hills,

The magnitude of human ills;

But neither could I know

To what full height our happiness can grow.

Sing, caged bird, sing !

Is this your constant strain?

I would, I would that I were free;

I would, I would, I would that I were once again

Sitting alone within a leafy tree;

I would that I might be

Breathing free air far from this gilded pain.

Ah, bird ! I would be free

As you, for I weary here.

And yet, my bird, I have one so dear, so dear,

That, if he might only bide with me,

I should no longer care

To change this stifling, fettered air

For the free mountain-breathings fresh and far.

Cold east and drear,

Your chill breath wraps the world in cheerless gray.

Sad east, while thou art here,

Life creeps with halting feet its weary way.

I feel you pierce my heart, oh, cold east wind !

Sad east ! that leavest lifeless plains behind.

The dull earth, watching, sleeps
Within her leafless bowers,
Until the west wind coming weeps
Soft tears that turn to flowers.
Oh, cruel east! that dost delay the world,
Withering the leaf of hope while yet unfurled.

Over this gray cheerless town
The yellow smoke-mist hangs, a squalid pall,
And night, too swift for springtide, settles down
Before the shades of mountain-evenings fall.
I sicken here alone, dull day by day,
To watch the turmoil wake and fade away.

Why does my dear not come,
Or write or send some little loving word?
It is not here as 'twas at home.
I have no companion but this prisoned bird;

No friend in all the throng to hear my sighs ;
No glance, but the cold stare of alien eyes.

No friend, nor love nor care
To hold me ; but when summer suns return
And wake this stagnant and exhausted air,
The little dearer life for which I yearn
May wake, and make me happier than of old,
Watching the innocent life my arms enfold.

Cold east and drear,
Spreading a noontide darkness on the town.
You shall not blight my faith, nor make me fear,
Nor leave me in despond, nor drag me down.
I am alone ; but, if he loves me still,
I am not all alone, sad days and chill.

SCENE III.

I grieve that my father stays away,

Though his letters are always dear and kind,

But sometimes I think they seem to convey

Some shadow of pain on a doubtful mind;

But he does not know that I am alone,

For I could not tell him my dear was gone,

And it may be he has not forgiven quite

Our foolish and hurried flight.

What?   Do I not know—forgive, did I say?—

That nought which falls short of committed wrong

Would keep his heart from his child for long,

Nought that a kiss would not chase away?

Dear father! I would I might welcome him here!

For, brooding here day by day,

My mind grows full of a formless fear,

And I dread the glance of the women; the sneer

Which I seem to see on their lips and eyes,

As they ask sometimes with a hard surprise

If my husband is ailing; he keeps away—

And I have but faltering words to say.

And to-day I thought, as I sate in my lonely room,

With a little frock on my lap, in the growing gloom,

And the woman came with the lights, that she seemed
   to look

With the old respect no more, but a cold rebuke.

Does she doubt, then, I am his wife? I will fly; I will go;

I will tell her all my secret.   Ah, no! ah, no!

Great Heaven, does she think he is gone and will no
   more come?

Oh, Henry, 'tis cruel to leave me, come to me, come
   home!   I

SCENE IV.

This is the fourth dull week—

I am wretched and sick at heart—

Since the thought came first which I fear to write or speak,

And I have no rest at night ; for I suddenly start,

Thinking I hear his voice calling to me in pain,

Mixed with voices of scorn sometimes, through the dead
    city-night ;

And then, if my tired eyes sink to slumber again,

I wake in deadly fright.

And before the bustle of life revives in the street,

I watch for the hurrying sound of the messenger's feet,

And I hold my breath as he comes with a sickening fear.

But the sharp summons passes on quickly, and never

    here

He comes; but I must not despair, nor ever forget

That I live for a ripening life, which 'twould injure to fret.

But I know that my face is pale and anxious and thin,

Which my love would hardly know, if he saw me again;

And I look in the glass, and I start to see therein

Two hollow eyes answer my gaze with a look of pain.

And perhaps he would love me no more in my beauty's

    disgrace;

Perhaps he was only a slave to a foolish face;

Perhaps——   But I know I am sick in body and mind,

Or I could not doubt my love, who was always kind.

My heart is heavy,

My life runs low,

My young blood's pulses

Beat faint and slow.

I cannot believe,

Yet I dare not doubt,

For when faith is shaken

Love's fire goes out.

Oh, Love, what is this

That thy strong power brings

To those thou hast touched

With thy fast-fleeting wings?

Oh, Love, it was cruel

To bring us to pain.

I will hide me away

From the cold world again.

I can stay here no longer;

Whatever may come,

I will go to my father

And—die at home.

My heart is heavy,

My life runs slow;

To my Father in Heaven

I open my woe.

SCENE V.

What is it that has been?
Let me once recall again
The fear that came upon me,
And the story of my pain.

Yester-eve, as I sat alone,
Somebody entered, and read
How the Earl, at some foreign bath,
Had been ailing and now was dead;

And pointed to the place,
And the letters seemed to swim,
And the whole room whirling round and round,
As my sight grew faint and dim.

For 'twas said that the new Earl,
His mourning done, would wed
The heiress of whom he told me before;
And I wished that I was dead.

And they muttered, with freezing glances,
" They had thought 'twas thus, before ; "
And I could not answer a single word,
But fell upon the floor.

And now I lie ailing and weak,
Sick in body and mind and heart ;
But to-morrow, if God help me,
I will rouse me and depart.

Oh, father, you will not spurn me,

Nor think me what they say,

But take us back to your heart and life,

And my grief shall fade away.

SCENE VI.

Oh, the sweet air of the hills,

That on this fair summer night

Breathes on me as I 'scape at last

From the glare of the long day,

From the dust of the long plain,

And the rushing, maddening train !

Here I mount among the pines

By the path we knew so well.

All is there unchanged but I.

Hark ! the thunder of the fall.

See the ash-grove where we sate.

There we lingered at the gate.

Nothing changed, but I am changed.

Slowly up the well-loved steep,

Failing footsteps toiling slow,

Where, upon the morning hills,

Twelve months since my feet would go

Bounding lightly as the roe.

None have seen me, that is well—

Yet if here I were to fail—

Courage ! I shall reach there—Nay,

I must rest awhile ; then climb

Slowly through the fragrant gloom,

Where my garden roses bloom.—

It is finished.   Dear white head

Bending low upon thy book,

Homely lamp, familiar room,

Ye will welcome me, I know.

Open, father ; I am come

Broken-hearted to my home !

ACT V.

SCENE I.] *Gwen.*

SCENE I.

GWEN.

It is over now.

I have been a long time ill,

But to-day I am able to wander slow

To the churchyard round the hill.

'Tis there they have laid my little love,

Who lingered three little months—it was not long—

And there they will lay me too, ere the waning light

    grows strong.

It is but a little grave

Where my little one is laid,

But I keep it decked with white flowers every day,

And above, a kindly yew's protecting shade

Shelters it safe from rain and wind.

Sleep fast, my darling, sleep while yet you may;

Your mother will not linger long behind.

Dear child, I wonder when

The last great morning breaks and we shall wake,

If I may bear you then

Safe in my nursing arms for Him to take;

Or will He suffer you to come before,

White soul, while I am waiting at the door?

Dear little grave, I strew

Fresh autumn flowers and garden blooms on you;

I strew upon you roses white and red;

I fling my heart upon you, narrow bed!

Once, twelve months since, I launched my heart, a rose,

Where, lit with laughter, Love's swift river goes,

And lo ! once more the year's swift pinions move,

And now I cast it on the grave of love.

My love, my self, my child,

Lie buried here, and I am free again.

I would I were a slave ; I loved my chain.

I would that I might see your sweet eyes mild ;

They were your father's eyes, who loves not me——

I blame him not, but do forgive for thee.

It is not long I stay, my life, my dear,

Not long until we are together here.

Last year—it seems an age ago—

I had not seen him : then we went

Together on our road ; and so,

By ways and converse innocent,

K

We gained at last the sacred gate
Of wedlock, and the hand of Fate
Lifted the latch, and we passed in
To the enchanted ground therein.
And now the winds of autumn rave,
And love lies dead within a grave.

Dear love, that liest there so still,
I go now till to-morrow's sun ;
The autumn evening gathers chill,
The day is well-nigh done.
Sleep, dear, through all thy long untroubled night,
Sleep calmly till the Light.

SCENE II.

What? Can a second springtide burst,

As happy as the first,

From out the midst of dark autumnal days?

And can the dead roots start?

And can the withered heart

Rise upward from despair to joy and praise?

Yes, though with thrills of almost pain,

They can, again.

For as I turned yesterday, sad and slow,

From where my darling lies below,

Fulfilled with sad sweet thoughts of the things that have

> been,

I saw my dear father's kindly face,

As he came to meet me with hurried pace,

And a grave smile that told me the news that he bore

> was good ;

But he slackened his steps when he saw me, and calmed

> his mood.

And I said, "Tell me all." And he answered, "'Tis well,

> my dear.

He was faithful ; I knew it, and is, for his letter is here,"

And he drew it forth ; and I knew that the writer was he,

And the title was that which he bears, and 'twas meant

> for me.

Then my father kissed my forehead and left me alone,

And I sat down to read what he said on a graveyard

> stone.

My love ! He too had been ill, for a chill he caught

When the Earl lay dying abroad, well-nigh brought him

    to nought ;

Growing to fevered heats and a wandering brain,

Till he raved for his nurse of last year to soothe him

    again ;

And when, after many days, he had risen to find

The wife he was forced to leave, with unquiet mind,

He found me not, but they said I had gone to my home.

And so, with loving regards, he promised to come,

Almost ere his letter could reach me.   Oh, love ! oh, my

    dear !

I shall see you again, though 'tis late ; and, meanwhile,

    a great fear

Rises up lest you grieve for your child whom you never

    have seen.

SCENE III.

He has come, he has been ;

I have kissed him again and again.

Ah, God ! but it is hard to die,

For it was not he was to blame at all, but I.

It was I, with my coward distrust and unreasoning fear,

Who could not put faith in my love, but shrank back
    from a sneer.

I am glad he was true throughout, though my sentence of
    doom

Sounds clear as I lie alone in my own white room.

To-day was a happy day,
When, upon my husband's breast,
I leaned beside the grassy mound
Where our firstborn lies at rest.

And we mutely went again
By the dear old paths once more,
And I half forgot my sorrow,
And the world was as before.

And he spoke with cheering words
Of the time when I should come

To cherish other children

In his old ancestral home.

Oh, my love as true as steel,

With your comfort kindly meant,

I would not seek to shadow

The light of your content;

But a hundred signs assure me,

Signs indefinite yet strong,

That my fate is wholly written

And I linger not for long.

Dearest, let us cling together,

Heart to heart and eye to eye;

Let us be together living,

And I shall not fear to die.

SCENE IV.

HENRY.

This is the last time that I tread

These unforgotten ways,

For to-morrow we follow the swallow over the wave.

We have spent our Mays;

Chill autumn has come and found us bent over a grave,

The grave of our youthful love and the hopes that are

     dead.

My dear, she is very pale and worn,

Save the brilliant spot that flushes on either cheek;

She recalls no longer the breezes and freshness of morn

As she leans upon me, slow and weak;

But I trust the warm summer sun and the honeyed air,

And the daily sights and sounds of things that are fair,

May rouse her and lighten her load of care.

Dear child ! to think of her pining alone,

While I lay longing for her and too weak to write,

And afraid to disclose by a look or a tone

The thing which discovered had wrecked us quite !

Ah, me ! 'twas a wretched time ; and now it is done,

My father is gone and my son, and I only remain,

Weak in frame, with a fading wife and a burden of
     pain.

Dear soul, I will do what by love and by gold can be
     done ;

I will bask with you safe from chill in the southern sun ;

And I pray that when summer returns and the meadows
     grow green,

You may sit in my stately home, as happy and proud as a
     queen.

But, oh ! what a fear is there

I dare not speak,

As I see the crimson deepen

On the pale wan cheek.

Nay, love, you are more lovely so,

A thousand times more fair,

Than when, twelve little months ago,

You went so free from care.

More dear you are, my love, and sweet,

A thousand times more dear,

Than when my heart forgot to beat

In the springtime of the year.

A thousand times more dear, my love,

A thousand times more dear,

For the tender pity that you move

And the anxious boding fear.

To-morrow, may it be

A new existence that we twain shall prove

Upon the western sea,

Bound for some happier land of health and love.

New hopes, new fears, new pains,

New joys; our hearts are ready, and we trust

The Omnipotent Will that reigns

Lifts not our hopes to dash them in the dust.

We hope; we cannot tell;

We go together alone, forgetting all;

For love, it shall be well,

Though life, a waning fire, may sink and fall.

Yet, if a prayer may move

Thy dread decrees, Omnipotent Will,

Spare, spare my innocent love

To my fond gaze a little longer still.

SCENE V.

GWEN.

Here is a calm bright day,
And my husband's tender voice;
He has climbed up from the village,
And I struggle to rejoice.

For I feel that to sorrow longer
For the little one who has fled,
My angel who rejoices
Among the blessèd dead,

Were a morbid grief, displeasing
To the Lord of joy and pain.

Nay, I will not sorrow longer ;
I will strive to live again.

To the beautiful far countries
Where the soft unfailing sun
Beams cloudless through the winter,
And the flowers are never done,

He will take me, undelaying,
Nought beside us, only me,
By the ship that leaves to-morrow
The great city on the sea ;

Every morning growing milder,
As we southward wing our way,
Till our swift ship casts her anchor
In some blue unruffled bay.

Stately cities I have read of,

Naples, Rome in all her pride—

I shall see them all, a great lady,

With my husband at my side.

I shall see them when returning

From the sacred stream of Nile,

From vast tombs of unknown rulers,

And the Sphinx's changeless smile.

I shall see them.   But in springtime,

When the bitter east is done,

I shall greet these dear old mountains

Shining in the sober sun ;

I shall see my father smiling ;

I shall bend once more again

O'er my sleeper's flower-strewed cradle,
Not with all unmingled pain.

I shall come, though, maybe sooner,
When I shall not see nor hear;
For my love has given his promise
I shall rest beside my dear.

—

Farewell, oh dear, dear hills !
I do not know if I shall see you more.
Farewell ! 'tis set of sun, the night is near.
Farewell !   Below, the mist of autumn fills
The sleeping vale with winding vapours frore,
And hides from sight the yellow woods and sere.

L

But on the heights the day's declining fire

Bathes all the summits in a haze of gold.

Not yet the cold mist, stealing high and higher,

Touches the purple glow with fingers cold;

Not yet the ruddy light from out the sky

Goes, nor the orange shadows fade and die.

Here, far above the grave of dying day,

The clear night comes, and hills and vales grow dark.

But soon the first faint star, a lucid spark,

Glimmers; and, lo! the ineffable array!

A myriad suns for one! strange suns and far,

The hidden homes where blessèd spirits are!

Oh, night of Being, like the night of day,

How should I fear because your shadows fall?

Who knows from what fresh glories thy dark pall

For failing vision lifts the veil away?

What boundless spiritual orbits rise

Before the inward gaze of dying eyes !

Farewell, oh little grave,

Wherein I leave my buried heart awhile !

Thick yew, protect it well until I come ;

Shelter it ; let not winds of winter rave,

Nor sharp frosts fret nor snows, nor floods defile.

Here is my heart, and here my waiting home.

Farewell ! farewell !

ACT VI.

SCENE I.

HENRY.

The sweet cold air of these untrodden hills

Breathes gently.   Five and twenty years have gone

Since here my father trod, young, high in hope,

With all the world before him ; nor as yet

The slow-consuming fire of deep decay

Had sapped his youthful hope, and left his life

To drag along its crippled journey, spent

In southern lands, wherever the chill cast

Might come not ; year by year : and last of all,

Since I have grown from boyhood, visiting

His country never; cut off and divorced

From all the joys that make existence sweet

To the aspiring great—the fame of men——

The name which every morning's broad-sheet takes

To the eyes and hearts of millions—all the thirst

For the statesman's high career swallowed and lost

In a strange lethargy which held him fast

In an inglorious case. And yet I know

A time there was when the more generous part

Allured his growing soul. For I have found

Among his papers, time-stained notes which tell

Of deeper studies far than I have dreamt of;

Of high hopes and ambitions; such as fire

Those who, as he and I, are placed by Fate

On such high vantage that to will alone

And labour is enough, and all the meed

Of place, the Senate itself, which opens not

To lower birth until slow-creeping age

Derides the folly, flings back early doors

To their unbroken youth.   These have I found.

And, oh most strange of all ! close manuscripts

Of sceptical themes—my father's, his who was,

Of all men I have known, most rapt by faith

And very full of Godhead—doubts and fears

And anxious questionings, changed yet the same,

Differing in form alone from those which now

At our own Oxford echo through old rooms

Filled with young heated disputants, whose minds

Take with a frolic eagerness the doubts

Which have perplexed all time.   All these I found.

Ah, life is wonderful !   We are the sport

Of great laws swinging slowly through an arc

Immeasurably vast.   We doubt our doubts,

We hug our faiths, and fancy we are free

Who are shut fast of Time.

                              What power it was

That checked his soul I know not, but sometimes

I think there must have come upon his life

Some overmastering passion, some young love

Such as the poets feign, for some young heart,

Which held him back and clogged him.   Yet I know—

I would stake my life upon it—naught of wrong

Came nigh him.   Only hardly love it was

That bound him to our mother—the high dame

He spoke of seldom, mourned seldomer still,

Whom scarcely I recall; whose clear cold face

Looks from beneath its coronet in my hall,

Statelier than any of our line.   Poor mother !

She left us early—me and little Gwen ;

Gwen, whom men know as Lady Gwendoline,

Our father's darling, who now comes with me

When hither, after years of exile spent

From home and homely scenes, we turn and leave

The turmoil of the Season and the chase

Of selfish worldlings, eager to secure

Those who are rich or fair.

                                        I had found of late,

Among our father's papers, reference

To this Welsh village, where, when he was young,

He spent a summer.   So we left behind

The senseless whirl, and for a week or more

In this unclouded weather, bright and fair,

We rove unchecked upon these purple hills

Where once our father, older scarce than I,

Roved in that far-off summer.   We have kept

Our name and rank a secret, and are free

To come and go at pleasure, as did he,

Dear father, years ago.   Ah ! sweet and strange,

The cycle of a life which turns and turns

Round to the self-same spot, changed yet the same

The same but for the mystic beat of Time ;

The same but for the ineffable change of Being,

Which in the same life, grown another, works

Infinite depths of change.

                    Somehow, I know not

If aught it be but fancy, but I think

The secret of his life, if such there were,

Lies hid within these hills ; and I remember

One day, when he was dying and his voice

Came feebler even than wont—the unruffled sea

Was sapphire, and the orange-groves behind

Showed flecked with gold—we heard a far-off bell

Call from the campanile on the hill,

And then he roused himself : " Hark ! 'tis the bell

From the dear church-tower on the hill above—

They both are there—'tis a fair spot—the path

Is steep from out the village, but the air

Is balmy—'tis the well-remembered bell—

They are singing now in Welsh, and the sound soothes

The sleepers by the yew."

And now they tell me

There is indeed a church on yonder hill,

A little church half hidden by dark yews,

Which looks upon the long green vale and scans

The ever-winding river.   So my sister,

Who learnt in Italy the sketcher's art,

Has gone before, armed with all fit devices

To snare the fleeting landscape.   It is time

To join her.   I must hasten ; it may be

(She is not strong, dear sister, but soon tires)

She tires of sketching and awaits me.   Father,

I would that you were with us, and might breathe

This sweet cold air again as young as I.

SCENE II.

GWEN.

How fair and fresh from this gray churchyard shows

The rich green vale beneath.   Upon the deep

Lush meadows, where the black herds grazing seem

Like rooks upon the grass, a silvery gleam,

Now lost and now discovered, marks the place

Where winds the brimming river.   Here, thick woods

Of oak and beech upon the sloping banks

Bend to the shadowy stream which glides beneath.

There, through the emerald meads, shallow or deep,

It hastes or loiters, till the tall dark elms

Grouped by the distance, hide it.   And above,

On either hand the eternal mountains rise,

Pine-clad below, upon whose upper heights

The unfenced heather purples.   All the sky

Is flecked with soft white fleecy clouds which throw

Bewildering charms of shadow; and beyond,

A shining azure drawn 'twixt earth and sky,

Glitters the summer sea.   Most beautiful

Thou art, oh motherland, which I have known

As yet so little.   Beautiful art thou

My second mother, sunny Italy,

Where the blue heaven is brighter, and the sea

Gives back a clearer azure.   But for me

There grows a tenderer charm from these green fields

And purple hills and white-flecked skies, denied

To thy more brilliant landscape.   Perhaps it is

In part because my father loved them well,

Dear father whom I loved, and who loved me

Closer than might a mother.

Well ! enough !
I will draw no more to-day, but let the scene
Sink on my soul, and fix itself, and breed
Fresh scenes of beauty to inspire my hand
When the short days are dull, and all the sky
A gloomy pall, and gusts of wintry rain
Beat on the darkling city.

                I will muse
A little till my brother comes, and think
How good he was whose memory brings us here ;
How careless of himself, how prompt to give
Whatever good a father's hand can give
To his motherless girl.   I scarcely had a thought
He did not share, and as I think, indeed,
He kept no secret from his earliest years
Of which I knew not.   He has told me all—
His studious youth, his feeble health, the doubt
Of God and man which for a while obscured

His noble brain and left it impotent—

And somehow it was here, upon these hills,

From out this very spot, it may be, gazing

On all the loveliness of earth and sky

And silver sea, the waters of his soul

Were loosèd, and flowed onward strong and clear,

To join the Infinite Deep !

                      There comes a cloud

Upon the sky and gusts of sudden wind ;

The beauty fades, as treacherous as youth,

And fleeting, and I thought I heard a roll

Of thunder drawing near.   I would my brother

Were come.   I am afraid.   The church is closed—

It is not here as 'tis in Italy,

Where all who choose may kneel as welcome guests

Within God's House ; but yon thick yew that stands

Above that gleaming cross will shelter me

From heavier storms than this.

                                    M

Here I am safe.

See with what tender care some loving hand

Keeps green the sward, and sets it round with flowers

That bloom as in a garden !   One red rose

Twines round the cross, and sheds in this rude wind

Its crimson petals.   Two graves stretch beneath,

And three sleep under.   Ah ! 'tis the old vicar's

Who lived here forty years and died last year.

" Also "—ah, see my brother comes at last—

" Also of "—strange, almost my name—" Gwenllian,

His daughter, who died aged twenty years "—

The year ?—one year before my father's marriage—

" Countess of "—What is this ?   My father's title !

Father, what means it ?—" And her infant son

Henry, Lord "—What, my brother's ?   What is this ?

It is strange.   Quick ! I am fainting . . .

Henry ! Henry

EPILOGUE.

The silent Forces of the World,

Time, Change, and Fate, deride us still;

Nor ever from the hidden summit, furled,

Where sits the Eternal Will,

The clouds of Pain and Error rise

Before our straining eyes.

It is to-day as 'twas before,

From the far days when Man began to speak,

Ere Moses preached or Homer sung,

Ere Buddha's musing thought or Plato's silvery tongue.

We pace our destined path with failing footsteps weak;

A little more we see, a little more

Of that great orb which shineth day and night

Through the high heaven, now hidden, now too bright,

The Sun to which the earth on which we are,
Life's labouring globe, is as the feeblest star.

Nor this firm earth we know
Which lies beneath our feet ;
Nor by what grades we have risen and shall grow,
Through chains of miracle, more and more complete ;
By what decrees the watery earth
Compacted grew the womb of countless birth ;
Nor, when the failing breath
Is taken by the frozen lips of Death,
Whither the Spoiler, fleeing with his prey,
The fluttering, wandering Wonder bears away.

The powers of Pain and Wrong,
Immeasurably strong,
Assail our souls, and chill with common doubt
Clear brain and heart devout :

War, Pestilence, and Famine, as of old,

The lust of the flesh, the baser lust of gold,

Vex us and harm us still ;

Fire comes, and crash and wreck, and lives are shed

As if the Eternal Will itself were dead ;

And sometimes Wrong and Right, the thing we fear,

The thing we cherish, draw confusedly near ;

We know not which to choose, we cannot separate

Our longing and our hate.

But Love the Conqueror, Love, Immortal Love,

Through the high heaven doth move,

Spurning the brute earth with his purple wings,

And from the great Sun brings

Some radiant beam to light the House of Life,

Sweetens our grosser thought, and makes us pure ;

And to a Higher Being doth mature

Our lower lives, and calms the ignoble strife,

And raises the dead life with his sweet breath,

And from the arms of Death

Soars with it to the eternal shore,

Where sight or thought of evil comes no more.

Love sitteth now above,

Enthroned in glory,

And yet hath deigned to move

Through life's sad story.

Fair Name, we are only thine !

Thou only art divine !

Be with us to the end, for there is none

But thou to bind together God and Man in one !

THE END.

PRINTED AT THE CAXTON PRESS, BECCLES.

THE EPIC OF HADES.

BOOK II. *

OPINIONS OF THE PRESS.

"Fresh, picturesque, and by no means deficient in intensity; but the most conspicuous merits of the author are the judgment and moderation with which his poem is designed, his self-possession within his prescribed limits, and the unfailing elegance of his composition, which shrinks from obscurity, exuberance, and rash or painful effort as religiously as many recent poets seem to cultivate such interesting blemishes. . . . . Perhaps the fine bursts of music in Marsyas, and the varied emotions portrayed in Andromeda, are less characteristic of the author than the prompt, yet graceful, manner in which he passes from one figure to another. . . . . Fourteen of these pieces written in blank verse which bears comparison with the very best models make up a thoroughly enjoyable little volume. . . . . Fully suited to maintain and crown the reputation the author has acquired by those which have preceded it."—*Pall Mall Gazette*, March 10th, 1876.

"It is natural that the favourable reception given to his 'Songs of Two Worlds' should have led the author to continue his poetical exercises, and it is, no doubt, a true instinct which has led him to tread the classic paths of song. In his choice of subject he has not shrunk from venturing on ground occupied by at least two Victorian poets. In neither case need he shrink from comparison. His Marsyas is full of fine fancy and vivid description. His Andromeda has to us one recommendation denied to Kingsley's—a more congenial metre; another is its unstrained and natural narrative."—*Saturday Review*, May 20th, 1876.

---

* Book II. was issued as a separate volume prior to the publication of Books I. and III. and of the complete work.

"In his enterprise of connecting the Greek myth with the higher and wider meaning which Christian sentiment naturally finds for it, his success has been great.   The passage in which Apollo's victory over Marsyas and its effect are described is full of exquisite beauty.   It is almost as fine as verse on such a subject could be. . . . . The little volume is delightful reading. From the first line to the last, the high and delicate aroma of purity breathes through the various spiritual fables."—*Spectator*, May 27th, 1876.

"The blank verse is stately, yet sweet, free, graceful, and never undignified.   We could have well wished that space had permitted us to make extracts.   We confidently believe that our readers will agree with us in regarding this as one of the finest and most suggestive poems recently published.   We trust to have, ere long, more poetic work from his hand."—*British Quarterly Review*, April 1st, 1876.

"The writer has shown himself more critical than his friends, and the result is a gradual, steady progress in power, which we frankly acknowledge. . . . . This long passage studded with graces."—*Academy*, April 29th, 1876.

"No lover of poetry will question his right to rank as a true poet.   His mark is made upon the age, and his future must be a matter of enduring interest."—*Sunday Times*, March 26th, 1876.

"From first to last, the work is that of a true poet, and such as a true poet alone could accomplish."—*Standard*, March 27th, 1876.

"Told as only a poet could tell such stories, with clearness of outline and chastity of colour : with rich, vivid imagination, always moulded and guided by an instinct of true artistic moderation and restraint ; with a pathos and a tenderness which bring home to us the loves and the sorrows even of those dim shades, and enable us to feel across the ages the quick throb of human brotherhood.   The world has to thank him for four volumes of true and exquisite poetry."   *Liverpool Albion*, March 18th, 1876.

"English blank verse of an exquisite sort, than which the Laureate himself pens none more perfect."—*Illustrated News*, May 27th, 1876.

THE EPIC OF HADES.

BOOKS I. and III. and the COMPLETE WORK.

OPINIONS OF THE PRESS.

"The author's present volumes continue the promise of his earlier work, and advance it somewhat further towards fulfilment. In one sense the idea of his Epic is not only ambitious but audacious, for it necessarily awakens reminiscences of Dante. Not unfrequently he is charmingly pathetic, as in his Helen and Psyche. There is considerable force and no small imagination in the description of some of the tortures in the 'Tartarus.' There is genuine poetical feeling in the 'Olympus.' . . . . We might invite attention to many other passages. But it is more easy to give honest general praise than to single out particular extracts."—*Times*, February 9th, 1877.

"The various symbolisms of the ancient myths are worked out with quite as much poetical feeling as in the former part. . . . . The whole of this last portion of the poem is exceedingly beautiful. . . . . Nor will any, except critics of limited view, fail to recognize in the Epic a distinct addition to their store of those companions of whom we never grow tired."—*Athenæum*, March 3rd, 1877.

"Clytemnestra is a striking dramatic study. . . . . The whole passage is as tragic as it is graphic. . . . . Thus the author has achieved the task he set himself of showing that the myths of classic antiquity are capable of interpretation by a modern singer. A simple, lucid style, a spontaneous power of song, and a bright, fearless fancy enable him to seize and retain the sympathies of his audience. We believe that the Epic will approve itself to students as one of the most considerable and original feats of recent English poetry."—*Saturday Review*, March 31st, 1877.

"We notice the same thoughtfulness and penetrating sympathy which have enabled the author, without doing violence to the sweet rounded grace of the old myths, to impart an undercurrent of present-day meaning and reference which should find for them a wider audience than could be expected for anything in the character of a severely Pagan revival merely. Thought, fancy, music, and penetrating sympathy we have here, and that radiant, unnamable suggestive delicacy which enhances the attraction with each new reading."—*British Quarterly Review*, April, 1877.

"The author most certainly possesses very great powers; but he is writing far too fast. We gladly repeat, however, that the present work is by far his greatest achievement; that the whole tone of it is noble, and that portions, more especially the concluding lines, are excessively beautiful."—*Westminster Review*, April, 1877.

"The work is one of which any singer might justly be proud. In fact, the Epic is in every way a remarkable poem, which to be appreciated must not only be read, but studied. It is that rarest of things, a book one would care to buy and keep."—*Graphic*, March 10th, 1877.

"This is in our opinion, in a high and serious sense, a remarkable poem—remarkable alike for thought, for music, and for fine suggestive quality. We look forward still to being made yet more the writer's debtors."—*Nonconformist*, February 21st, 1877.

"All his poems have proved him appreciative, thoughtful, and scholarly. 'The Epic of Hades' should rank highest of his work."—*Examiner*, February 24th, 1877.

"We do not hesitate to advance it as our opinion that 'The Epic of Hades' will enjoy the privilege of being classed amongst the poems in the English language which will live."—*Civil Service Gazette*, March 17th, 1877.

"Exquisite beauty of melodious verse. . . . . A remarkable poem, both in conception and execution. We sincerely wish for the author a complete literary success."—*Literary World*, March 30th, 1877.

"The author never sinks low, but he often rises high, and thus you have poetry which pleases you as you read, which shocks no sensibility, never wearies you, and often raises you into a serener atmosphere, in which the earthiness of the earth is lost sight of, and the pure and almost the divine are found. It will be surprising if the reader does not come to the conclusion that the author is a poet of very high order."—*Scotsman*, April 27th, 1877.

" Will live as a poem of permanent power and charm. It will receive high appreciation from all who can enter into its meaning, for its graphic and liquid pictures of external beauty, the depth and truth of its purgatorial ideas, and the ardour, tenderness, and exaltation of its spiritual life."—*Spectator*, May 5th, 1877.

" I have lately been reading a poem which has interested me very much, a poem called 'The Epic of Hades.' Many of you may never have heard of it ; most of you may never have seen it. It is, as I view it, another gem added to the wealth of the poetry of our language."—*Mr. Bright's speech on Cobden at Bradford*, July 25th, 1877.

" I have derived from it a deep pleasure and refreshment such as I never thought modern poetry could give."—*The Bishop of Gloucester and Bristol*.

"This poem is not in the merely technical sense an epic, any more than the divine poem of Dante is a comedy. That was a comedy, as passing to a happy close ; from Hell, through Purgatory, into Paradise. This is an epic, as it is concerned with one great action ; for the soul of man is shown throughout it labouring towards what Mr. Tennyson has called the

> One far-off divine event
> To which the whole Creation moves.

In the blank verse of the 'Epic of Hades,' apt words are so simply arranged with unbroken melody, that if the work were printed as prose, it would remain a song, and every word would still be where the sense required it ; not one is set in a wrong place through stress of need for a mechanical help to the music. The poem has its sound mind housed in a sound body."—*Professor Morley in The XIXth Century*, February, 1878.

THESE poems were originally published in three volumes, issued in the years 1872, 1874, and 1875. The following are a few selections from the Press notices which appeared as they were issued.

(FIRST SERIES.)

"No one after reading the first two poems—almost perfect in rhythm and all the graceful reserve of true lyrical strength—could doubt for an instant that this book is the result of lengthened thought and assiduous training in poetic forms. These poems will assuredly take high rank among the class to which they belong."—*British Quarterly Review*, April, 1872.

"If this volume is the mere prelude of a mind growing in power, we have in it the promise of a fine poet. . . . . In 'The Wandering Soul,' the verse describing Socrates has that highest note of critical poetry, that in it epigram becomes vivid with life, and life reveals its inherent paradox. It would be difficult to describe the famous irony of Socrates in more poetical and more accurate words than by saying that he doubted men's doubts away."—*Spectator*, February 17th, 1872.

"Throughout there is the true lyrical note, the 'cry' that seems to veil itself in the harmony of the language it chooses, and so makes itself only the more imperatively felt. Seldom, indeed, does it fall to the lot of the critic to come on such a prize as this. . . . . No extracts could do justice to the exquisite tones, the felicitous phrasing and delicately wrought harmonies of some of these poems."—*Nonconformist*, March 27th, 1872.

"In all this poetry there is a purity and delicacy of feeling which comes over one like morning air."—*Graphic*, March 16th, 1872.

(SECOND SERIES.)

"In earnestness, sweetness, and the gift of depicting nature, the writer may be pronounced a worthy disciple of his compatriot, Henry Vaughan, the Silurist. Several of the shorter poems are instinct with a noble purpose and a high ideal of life. One perfect picture, marginally annotated, so to speak, in the speculations which it calls forth, is 'The Organ-Boy.' But the most noteworthy poem is the 'Ode on a Fair Spring Morning,' which has somewhat of the charm and truth to nature of ' L'Allegro and Il Penseroso.' It is the nearest approach to a master-piece in the volume."—*Saturday Review*, May 30th, 1874.

"If in any respect this second series is superior to the first, it is in a certain mellowness and warmth of tone. The poem entitled 'To an Unknown Poet' is a wonderful combination of insight, melody, picture, and suggestion. 'The Organ-Boy' brings out a strong contrast in a most powerful and felicitous way."—*British Quarterly Review*, July 1st, 1874.

"This volume is a real advance on its predecessor of the same name, and contains at least one poem of great originality, as well as many of much tenderness, sweetness, and beauty. 'The Organ-Boy' we have read again and again, with fresh pleasure on every reading. It is as exquisite a little poem as we have read for many a day."—*Spectator*, June 13th, 1874.

"The reception of the New Writer's first series shows that, in his degree, he is one of the poetical forces of the time. Of the school of poetry of which Horace is the highest master, he is a not undistinguished pupil."—*Academy*, August 11th, 1874.

"This series is superior to the first. No person of the least sensitiveness could read a few pages of this volume, and deny that the writer possesses the 'vision of the poet.' The glance, the touch, the hint suffice, and you have not only a picture, but a series of pictures. Of the poems we can only say that they are quick with wisdom and high thought, touched with phantasy, and flowing easily into imaginative forms."—*Nonconformist*, June 24th, 1874.

"A warm welcome is due to this pleasant and able volume of poems, which is marked by distinctness of aim, artistic clearness of execution, and that particular imaginative lustre which belongs to the truly poetic mind."—*Guardian*, September 20th, 1874.

"The verses are full of melodious charm, and sing themselves almost, without music."—*Blackwood's*, August 1st, 1874.

(THIRD SERIES.)

"Not unworthy of its predecessors. It presents the same command of metre and diction, the same contrasts of mood, the same grace and sweetness. It cannot be denied that he has won a definite position among contemporary poets."—*Times*, October 16th, 1875.

"'Evensong' shows power, thought, and courage to grapple with the profoundest problems. In the 'Ode to Free Rome' we find worthy treatment of the subject and passionate expression of generous sympathy."—*Saturday Review*, July 31st, 1875.

"More perfect in execution than either of its predecessors. . . . . The pure lyrics are sweeter and richer. In the 'Birth of Verse' every stanza is a little poem in itself, and yet a part of a perfect whole."—*Spectator*, May 22nd, 1875.

"'Evensong' is a poem in which the source of inspiration is the sublimity to which thought is led by the contemplation of metaphysical problems. It would be impossible to give any notion of the poem by quotations."—*Athenæum*, May 8th, 1875.

"It would be well, indeed, if our more successful versifiers as a rule fulfilled their early promise as calmly, equably, and melodiously as the author. His range of moral sympathy is large, and his intellectual view is wide enough to embrace a great variety of subjects."—*Guardian*, September 1st, 1875.

"If each book that he publishes is to mark as steady improvement as have his second and third, the world may surely look for something from the writer which shall immortalize him and remain as a treasure to literature."—*Graphic*, June 1st, 1875.

"The author's healthiness and uprightness of feeling refresh one like a cold air after a hot and sultry day. 'The Home Altar' should in future adorn every collection of English religious verse. . . . . The exquisite cadence of these verses. . . . . The farewell that he threatens cannot be permitted."—*Examiner*, May 8th, 1875.

"The high hopes we had been led to entertain are here realized. . . . . At one page he is celebrating the doubts bred of science, and on the next the poor little 'Arabs,' enlisted in the sale of the cheap newspapers, have due celebration, and that more successfully than was even the case with that wonderful poem in the last volume, 'The Organ-Boy.' We despair of doing justice to this choice volume by extract."—*Nonconformist*, May 19th, 1875.

www.ingramcontent.com/pod-product-compliance
Lightning Source LLC
Chambersburg PA
CBHW022353020726
47500CB00002B/248